APRIL PULLEY SAYRE

THANK YOU, EARTH

A LOVE LETTER TO OUR PLANET

 GREENWILLOW BOOKS, *AN IMPRINT OF* HarperCollins*Publishers*

Dear Earth,

Thank you for water
and those that float,

for slippery
seaweed

and stone.

Thank you for mountains and minerals,

that strengthen bills

and bone.

Thank you for air—

even fishy whale breath.

Thank you for colors and coastlines

and beach.

Thank you for tiny

and towering.

For trees

and
vines
that
reach.

Thank you for curves

and prickles

and parallels.

For patterns—

all shapes that repeat.

Thank you for leaves

and stems
and buds,

for plant parts

we can eat.

Thank you
for sounds

and storms,

and seasons.

For struggles—

and pale
in-betweens.

Thank you for rays
and radials,

and overlapping greens.

Thank you for jumbles—
ingredients for soil

and bright

new growth in spring.

Thank you for those that crawl.

Yes, all.

All.

All.

Even for those that sting.

Thank you
for sunsets.

For
edges
eyes
can
roam.

Thank you for beginnings,

for endings,

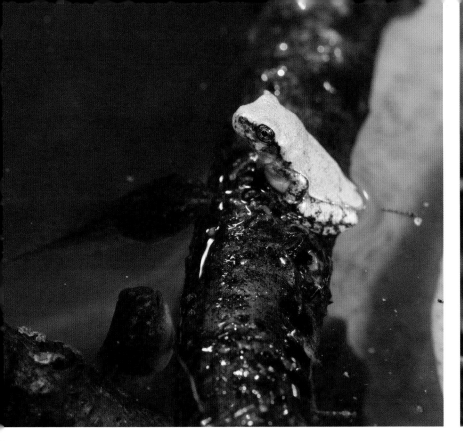

for lifetimes.

Thank you
for being

our home.

A NOTE FROM THE AUTHOR

This book is a thank-you note to the earth. The earth provides us with so much. Earth's atmosphere gives us air to breathe. Our planet gives us food to eat and water to drink. Minerals in the earth—calcium and magnesium—strengthen our teeth and bones. Earth is the ground we walk on, the place we live, our home.

The earth itself does not have an address to receive thank-you notes. But writing thank-you notes, even to clouds or rivers or continents, can still help the planet. By sharing thank-you words and art, we can remind one another about what nature does for us. This will encourage all of us to remember Earth in our actions, to protect the planet, and to spread the message of caring and conservation.

So, how do you send thank-you notes to a planet? Share your notes with others through hallway art in your school. Mail your thank-you notes to newspapers, magazines, and television stations in your school and in your community. Send them to elected officials. Think big. Your thank-you notes can be any size, shape, color, or format—even video.

Turn a thank you into action

Kids all over the earth are transforming their thank yous into action, too. In Michigan, students at Whitehall Middle School are asking kids to participate in National Skip the Straw Day. They are asking schools not to use straws. They are asking kids, when they go to restaurants, to request that the waiter NOT automatically bring straws to the table. Straws are plastic and made for a single use. Hundreds of millions are used and thrown away every day. And plastic is filling landfills and polluting the ocean, endangering birds, sea turtles, dolphins, and whales.

In Ohio, a student named Delaney had a question: why is littering the sky okay when we discourage littering on the ground? Delaney searched for, retrieved, and reported stray balloons along the Lake Erie shoreline. She called and wrote letters to ask people not to litter the sky by releasing hundreds of balloons during celebrations. These balloons drift many miles and often land as trash in waterways and the ocean. The deflated balloons make a mess and kill birds and mammals.

Perhaps some other Earth issue is pressing and important in your community. Here are ideas for ways to get started with putting your thank you into action:

Investigate the facts

Learn where your drinking water comes from.

Learn about air quality in your community—what makes the air cleaner some days than others. Learn about the weather and the climate where you live, and where your rainwater goes.

Learn where your electricity and heat come from. How are they generated?

Learn how and where the everyday products you use—from computers to writing paper—are made. Who makes them? What are the ingredients?

Learn where what you throw away goes. How is your garbage disposed of?

Share the story

Speak. Write. Photograph. Draw. Create posters, videos, essays, and other things to share what you have learned with your friends and classmates.

Inspire others to think differently about the earth and what it provides for all of us.

Participate

Help at a beach or river cleanup day.

Plant trees.

Create a wildlife garden, and support wildlife in your area. Plant native plants that

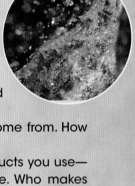

feed and shelter birds, butterflies, and other creatures.

Conserve energy, paper, cloth, and food—products that require materials, including fresh water, to make. By conserving you are leaving more water, materials, and space for wildlife.

Be an inventor

Study, brainstorm, and design new ways to conserve resources, and help wildlife and the planet.

Help the helpers

Some of the issues facing Earth may be beyond your neighborhood, in places that need professionals, including scientists, on site to do the helping work. How can you assist?

Find out about organizations that work on these conservation issues. Raise money to help support them. Send thank-you notes to encourage their work. Ask others, including government officials, to help them.

Ask for action

Write to elected officials and companies to let them know that you care about Earth issues. Ask them to take action to help the earth. And send a thank-you note when they do take action to help.

You have a voice. Gather friends to help. Speak out and share. Young people, especially those who investigate the facts and become informed about an issue, can change the world.

SELECT RESOURCES AND ORGANIZATIONS

Jane Goodall's Roots & Shoots ● www.rootsandshoots.org
This organization, part of the Jane Goodall Institute, is focused on helping young people, even very young children, create and carry out Earth-helping actions.

Authors for Earth Day ● www.authorsforearthday.org
These children's book authors visit schools and empower kids by donating to help Earth charities chosen by students.

Balloons Blow ● www.balloonsblow.org
This organization, founded by two sisters, educates about plastic pollution and encourages people not to do balloon releases.

Sea Turtle Conservancy ● www.conserveturtles.org
This organization has kid-friendly programs to protect and monitor sea turtle nesting beaches.

National Wildlife Federation ● www.nwf.org
National Wildlife Federation (NWF) publishes *Ranger Rick* and *Ranger Rick Jr.* They have a wildlife gardening program, a butterfly heroes program, and an eco-schools program.

Monarch Watch ● www.monarchwatch.org
This is the major monarch tracking and conservation program in the United States.

The 5 Gyres Institute ● www.5gyres.org
"More ocean, less plastic," is the motto of this organization that educates about and works to help solve the plastic pollution problem worldwide.

American Bird Conservancy ● www.abcbirds.org
This organization advocates for legislation to help birds, and protects the winter habitat of warblers and other birds in the tropics.

The Nature Conservancy ● www.nature.org
This organization protects the habitats of varied and rare plants and animals.

World Wildlife Fund ● www.worldwildlife.org
This organization works on wildlife issues, especially endangered species and habitats worldwide.

ACKNOWLEDGMENTS

To my sisters, Cathy and Lydia. Thank you, Candace & George, Gil & Laura, Ken & Patti, Barb & John, Rodney, John, Liz, Virginia, John David, Catherine, Winston, Nora, Turner, Tom, Harlow, Pearl, Ann, Carolyn, Michael, Chris, Becky, Megan, Karyn, and Isabel. Thank you, Raúl Arias de Para, Carlos Bethancourt, and Jenn Sinasac of the Canopy Tower family; Jamie Hogan; South Bend Farmer's Market; Karen Romano Young; JoAnn Early Macken; Liz Cunningham; the Hive, Healing Earth, and the Hunt family. Love to my favorite earthling, my husband, Jeff. (Thanks for the elk and for driving 5,000 miles.)

PHOTOGRAPHS ● FRONT COVER

T: sunrise over Lake Michigan, Chicago, Illinois; H: eggplant, South Bend Farmer's Market, Indiana; A: flower petals, Indiana; N: leafhopper, Indiana; K: abalone shell, Florida; Y: red milkweed beetle; Earth, Vitalij Cerepok/EyeEm/Getty Images; U: philodendron leaf, Ohio; comma: sand, White Sands National Monument, New Mexico; E: sandhill cranes, Medaryville, Indiana; A: hickory trees/sunset, Indiana; R: brown pelican, Florida; T: window raindrops, St. Patrick's County Park, South Bend, Indiana; H: sunflower, Indiana

PHOTOGRAPHS ● INTERIOR

1: female mallard in water reflecting autumn maple trees, Indiana. 2-3: spider web on chicory plant, Peaks Island, Maine; long-billed curlew, Moss Landing Wildlife Area, California; Caribbean Sea. 4-5: sea otter, Monterey, California; white ibis and willet, Fort Myers, Florida; kelp, Monterey, California; seaweed and stones, Peaks Island, Maine. 6-7: mountains and red sandstone formations, Arches National Park, Utah; Common raven, Colorado; elk, Neal Smith National Wildlife Refuge, Iowa. 8-9: airplane view; fin whales, Saguenay–St. Lawrence Marine Park, Quebec, Canada; Pictured Rocks National Lakeshore, Michigan; harbor seals, Fitzgerald Marine Reserve, California. 10-11: lady beetle, Indiana; maple tree, Warren Dunes State Park, Michigan. 12-13: spruce-fir forest, White Mountain National Forest, New Hampshire; three-toed sloth in cecropia tree, Canopy Tower, Soberanía National Park, Panama; Virginia creeper vine on American beech tree, Lincoln, New Hampshire. 14-15: Echevaria species, Seal Cove Inn garden, Moss Beach, California; saguaro, Tucson, Arizona; red-banded leafhoppers on cup plant, South Bend, Indiana; green sea turtle hatchlings, Seven Mile Beach, Cayman Islands. 16-17: cultivated sunflower, South Bend, Indiana; native downy sunflowers, Prairie Oaks Metro Park, Columbus, Ohio. 18-19: oak leaves, Fernwood Botanical Garden and Nature Preserve, Michigan; wild lupine and ant, Indiana; carrot and eggplant, South Bend Farmer's Market, Indiana. 20-21: yellow warbler, Ottawa National Wildlife Refuge, near Toledo, Ohio; storm, Englewood, Florida; black oak in snow, Indiana; eastern fox squirrel on pussy willow, Indiana. 22-23: black-crowned night heron, Venice Area Audubon Rookery, Florida; morning ocean, Lemon Bay Aquatic Preserve, Florida; dark-eyed junco on pussy willow, Indiana. 24-25: native bee on purple coneflower, Indiana; dandelion, South Carolina; ferns and hosta, South Bend, Indiana; 26-27 mushroom and maple leaves, Connecticut; eastern redbud tree, Indiana; bloodroot flower, Indiana. 28-29: red mangrove root crab, Dominican Republic; black swallowtail caterpillar on dill, Indiana; ants on globe thistle, Indiana; bold jumping spider, Dianthus flower, Michigan; skipper and honeybees on globe thistle, Indiana. 30-31: saguaro and sunset, Phoenix Sonoran Preserve, Arizona. 32-33: sandhill cranes, Jasper-Pulaski Fish and Wildlife Area, Medaryville, Indiana; natural red sandstone formation, Arches National Park, Utah. 34-35: toad eggs, Indiana; cannonball jelly, Jacksonville, Florida; gray tree frogs, Indiana; cottontail rabbit, Indiana; wood duck, Indiana. 36-37: eastern fox squirrel, Indiana; penstemon flowers, Tucson, Arizona; beach, Manasota Key, Florida. 40: halictid bee and flower spider on great blue lobelia.

AUTHOR'S NOTE PHOTOS

Background: sky, Indiana. Earth, Vitalij Cerepok/EyeEm/Getty Images; fin whales, Quebec, Canada; green sea turtles, Grand Cayman; stream water, Indiana; carrots, Indiana; fall tree, Williamsburg, Virginia; honeybee on aster, Indiana; American toads, South Bend, Indiana; dragonfly, Potato Creek State Park, Indiana; yellow warbler, Ohio; wood stork, the Alligator Farm, St. Augustine, Florida; pelicans, Englewood, Florida; lady beetle, Indiana.

For all who feel the same way
—A. P .S.